The Fatal Secret

The Fatal Secret

Or, Constancy in Distress

Eliza Haywood

MINT EDITIONS

The Fatal Secret: Or, Constancy in Distress was first published in 1725.

This edition published by Mint Editions 2021.

ISBN 9781513291598 | E-ISBN 9781513294445

Published by Mint Editions®

 MINT
EDITIONS

minteditionbooks.com

Publishing Director: Jennifer Newens
Design & Production: Rachel Lopez Metzger
Project Manager: Micaela Clark
Typesetting: Westchester Publishing Services

Nothing is so generally coveted by Womankind, as to be accounted Beautiful; yet nothing renders the Owner more liable to Inconveniences. She who is fond of Praise, is in great Danger of growing too fond of the Praiser; and if by chance she does defend herself from the Attacks made on her *Virtue*, it is almost a Miracle if her *Reputation* receives no Prejudice by them: And a Woman who is very much admir'd for the Charms of her *Face*, ought with infinitely more Reason be so for those of her *Prudence*, who preserves both amidst so many Enemies as Love and Opportunity will raise against them. For one Woman that has made her Fortune by her Beauty, there are a thousand whose utter Destruction it has been.—Some, among a Crowd of Adorers, are so long determining which shall be the happy Man, that Time stealing everyday away some Part of their Attractions, they grow at last depriv'd of all, and on a sudden find themselves abandon'd, and not worth a Bow from those whose Hearts and Knees bended at their Approach before.—Others, puzzled with a too great Variety, have their Judgments dimm'd with the Confusion of Ideas, and more frequently make Choice of the worst than the contrary.—A third Sort there are, who, by becoming a publick Toast, assume to themselves such an Air of Insolence and Self-sufficiency, that their Behaviour forfeits the Conquest which their Eyes had gain'd, and they grow in a little Time rather Objects of Ridicule than Admiration.—Numberless are the Dangers to which a young Creature, more than ordinarily fair, is incident; and even where there is the greatest Stock of Virtue, Modesty, and good Sense, it sometimes is the Occasion of Misfortunes which are not to be warded off by all those Guard.

Anadea, the only Daughter of a Gentleman of high Extraction, but mean Fortune, in *Paris* was so much celebrated for her exceeding Beauty, that it grew almost a Proverb; and it was a common Saying, when anyone would praise a Lady, to cry, She is as handsome as *Anadea!* as fine shap'd as *Anadea!*—Nor were the Charms of her Conversation less amiable than those of her Person: Her indulgent Father, though in his Youth he had lavish'd the best Part of his Patrimony, and had little to depend on but what accrued from a Post he held at Court, was now so good a Husband in other Things, as to afford her a very liberal Education. There was no Accomplishment fit for a young Lady, that she was not Mistress of; and she made such good Use of her Time, that before she arrived at the Age of Sixteen, she acquir'd more than the most ingenious of her Fellow-Learners could do at Twenty four.

Nor confin'd she her Studies to that Part of Education common to her own Sex: She had an extensive Genius, and emulated the other in their Search of Knowledge; she went a great ways in the Mathmaticks; understood several Languages perfectly well; and had she presever'd in Application, might have been as eminent for her Learning, as the celebrated Madam *Dacier:*

But she being now a Woman, and her Father's Age, and some Infirmities incident to it, making him believe he had not long to live, and consequently desirous of seeing his beloved Child dispos'd of before his Death, induced him to entertain her often with Discourse of Marriage. He was continually pressing her to let him know which, of the many who had offer'd themselves, was most agreeable to her Mind; but finding her Inclinations far from being as he desired, and that she rather seem'd to listen to such Conversations through Obedience to him, than any Liking to change her condition, he grew extremely chagrin'd at it, and at last told her, that he was resolved on her Marriage, and as his Indulgence had prevail'd upon him to give her the Choice of which of her Admirers should be Man, he expected she should, without any farther Evasions, determine. This was the first Shock *Anadea* had ever found to ruffle her Calm of Life; but, unable to stand it, well knowing her Father, in spite of all the Tenderness he had for her, was not of a Humour to endure Disobedience in those he had Power over, answered him in this Manner.—Since 'tis your Pleasure, Sir, that I must be a Wife, I shall endeavour to conquer my Inclinations, which I confess tend to a single Life; but as it is your Place to command, and mine to obey, I beg you will exert that Power in everything; direct me to whom I must resign my Liberty, and I shall yield with as little Reluctance as Nature will permit. These Words were not perfectly pleasing to him they were address'd to; he loved her too well, to oblige her to do anything to which she was averse; and to perswade her that it was wholly for her Interest to marry, omitted no Arguments which he thought might be conducive to that End: He represented to her the Dangers of a young Woman's being left alone in the World, expos'd both to Temptations and Insults; and reminded her, that when he was gone, how impossible it would be for her to support herself in the Manner she had liv'd, in so moving a Strain, and expressed so tender a Grief that he was unable to leave her a Fortune suitable to her Birth, and the Education he had given her, that she had no longer anything to reply in Contradiction to the Justice of what he alleg'd; and if she was not in reality convinced, she chose to appear so, rather than bear to see the Sorrows which his paternal Care, and soft Commiseration for the Apprehension of what Misfortunes she might fall into, involved him in—She assured him at last, that she was perfectly easy, and ready to fulfil his Commands; but as to the Choice of a Husband, begg'd he would not leave it to her, telling him, with a great deal of Sincerity, that as she had no particular *Aversion* to any Man, so among the Number of those who had made Pretensions, she was not capable of feeling any particular *Regard*, but would endeavour to increase a Respect for him who he should think most worthy. The Old gentleman, finding himself oblig'd to name the Person, was not much less at a Loss than his Daughter, for there were several of equal Merit who aim'd at the Blessing of obtaining her: However, thinking he had done enough for once, in getting her Consent to marry, he deferred letting her know to whom, till another Time.—But it was not many Days before the Chevalier *De Samar* gain'd the Advantage of all his Rivals.—He was descended from a very noble Family, which was no small Recommendation to the Father of *Anadea*, had a handsome Estate, and was a Gentleman of known Sobriety and good Conduct.— He was the Person fix'd on; and *Anadea*, when she heard it, having nothing to offer in Opposition, the o'erjoyed Lover was soon made acquainted with the Happiness designed him, and everything was getting ready with all possible Expedition for the Solemnity. The Time which the necessary Preparations took up, *Anadea* pass'd in modelling her Soul, as much as possible, to be pleas'd with the State for which she was intended.—The *Chevalier* had many good Qualities, and she endeavoured to add to them in Imagination a thousand more. Never did any Woman take greater Pains to resist the Dictates of Desire, than she did to create them: But, alas! she had not yet seen those Charms which were necessary to inspire the Passion which alone could make the Loss of her beloved Liberty a Blessing: And though she joined in that Opinion she found the whole World had of him, that her intended Husband was a perfect fine Gentleman, yet she had it not in her Power to feel any of those soft Emotions, those Impatiencies for his Absence, those tender Thrillings in his Presence, nor any of those agreeable Perplexities which are the unfailing consequences of Love; and without which she was sensible, both by Reading, and her own Observation on others, there could be no true Extasies in Possession. Not all his Assiduity, not all his Tenderness, not all her own Efforts, could bring her to anymore than to be barely satisfied with her Lot; and she began, at length, to lay the Blame on her own want of Sensibility, and to imagine she had not a Heart fram'd like those of other Women.—Happy, at least contented, might she have been, had she never had Cause to change her Sentiments. But soon, too soon, the luckless Moment came, which was to convince her, that of all her Sex, none was more capable of receiving a soft Impression, nor, for all her Knowledge, none less able to repel it.

Hap'ning to be one Evening at the House of a young Lady of her particular Acquaintance, the Count *Blessure*, Son to a Marquis of that Name, being lately arriv'd at *Paris*, whence he had been absent sometime on his Travels, made his visit there at the same Time. It was the Sight of him that first gave her to know there was a Possibility for her to wish to be a Wife, and if her design'd Husband had been like him, she might, with equal Ardour, equal Impatiency, have long'd for the happy Hour which should resign her to him.—The Count, indeed, had everything which could excuse a Woman's sudden Liking; for besides the Charms of his Person, (which were hardly to be equall'd,) there was something irresistibly engaging in his Conversation;—something so very graceful, yet withal so sweet, that it was almost an Impossibility to be in his Company without being more than ordinarily pleas'd with it:—But, beside the Attractions he had for the Generality of those who knew him, all his Notions and Sentiments of Things, and his Manner of expressing what he thought, were more particularly adapted to move the Soul of *Anadea*;—He had an uncommon Delicacy in his Nature; so had she:—A grave Chearfulness, or, if you will, a gay Solidity in his Behaviour; so had she.—In fine, never were two Persons of different Sexes so alike, so fram'd to please each other.—The natural Boldness of Manhood was in him sweetly temper'd with a more than female Softness; and the Tenderness and Bashfulness incident to Womankind, in her was mingled with something of a manly majesty of Thought, commanding what she perswaded, while he seemed to beseech what he enforc'd.—Both were so equally enflamed by each other, that 'tis hard to say which had the Start in the great Race of Passion. Yet neither Heart was sensible of its Happiness; for though both were so much accustomed to charm, that it was almost as common to be ador'd as to be seen, yet the prodigious Awe which Love always inspires, kept either from believing they had had the Power of conquering here.

Cards being proposed by the Lady of the House, they went to *Ombre*; but little were the *Count* or *Anadea* capable of managing their Game: Never was such distracted Playing; they threw away their *Matadores*, and *Punto* was no more remember'd. They play'd on however, and *Anadea*, quite lost in Thought and Contemplation, forgot the Time of Night, and thought not of removing till the *Chevalier*, having some Hours waited for her coming home, in hope of paying his Devoirs, was sent by her Father, to see the Reason of her staying abroad so much later than she had been accustomed.—His Entrance rouz'd both these amiable Persons from the pleasing Dreams they had been in: *Anadea*, seeing them together, had the greater Opportunity of making a Comparison between them; but, Oh! she found there was non!—This new Charmer had in everything the Advantage!—And though the *Chevalier* was a Man who might justly be accounted very agreeable, yet in the Presence of the unequall'd *Blessure*, he had nothing which seemed worthy Consideration! How destructive to her Peace was now her Delicacy of Taste, and penetrating Judgment! She now knew there was something more excellent in Man than she had imagined; but at the same Time knew the Discovery promised nothing but Despair. She was pre-engaged to another by all the binding Vows that Words could form; and if he should happen to regard her with Eyes of Love, which yet was not in her Thoughts, it was not in her Power to gratify his or her own Desires. The *Count* was in little less Perplexity; he easily perceived by the Freedom with which the *Chevalier* entertained her, that he was a Lover publickly allow'd; and though till after they had taken Leave he knew not how far the Matter had gone, yet he immediately suspected enough to make him sensible what kind of galling grinding Pains those are which Jealousy inflicts.

In Anxieties, such as hopeless Lovers feel, did the discontented *Anadea* pass the Night:—She could not avoid wishing, though there was not the least room for her to imagine a Possibility of what she wish'd:—She could not help praying, yet thought those Prayers a Sin.—Her once calm and peaceful Bosom was now all Hurry and Confusion:—the Esteem which she had been long labouring to feel for the *Chevalier*, was now turn'd to Aversion and Disdain; and the Indifference she had for all Mankind, now converted into the most violent Passion for one.—Far from imagining what Effect her Charms had wrought on the lovely Object of her new Desires, she thought she could be contented to live a single Life, and knew so little of the encroaching Nature of the Passion she had entertained, that she believed she should never languish for any greater Joy, than that she might, without a Crime, indulge Comtemplation with the Idea of his Perfections; and to destroy that pleasing Theory by marrying with another, whom them she could not, without failing in her Duty, rob of one single Wish, was more terrible to her than the worst of Deaths.—confounded what to do, or rather wild that there was nothing she *could* do that might be of Service to her in an Exigence like this, her Mind grew all chaos, and the unintermitting Inquietudes of her Soul not permitting any repose, she was so much disorder'd the next Day, that she had a very good Pretence to keep her Chamber, and receive no Visits.—If a Person in her Condition ever finds Ease, 'tis when they are alone; for Company, Noise, and Hurry, though they are ordinary Recipe's for Melancholy, are so far from working the Effect they are design'd for, that, on the contrary, they but increase the Malady: Love and Grief are Passion too potent to be struggled with, and too obstinate for Perswasion:—Opposition makes them mad:—They grow fiercer by Restraint:—The patient is himself his own best Physician; and if by soothing his Disease he does not absolutely cure it, he, at least, prevents the Tortures it would otherwise occasion: And it has been often seen, that in giving a Loose to the Passion, the Spirit had evaporated of itself; though this never happens but in a weak and flashy Mind, and could not be the case of our *Anadea*. As she was not easily wounded by the Darts of Love, so having once received them, could not suffer them to be torn out, without breaking at the same Time the strings of Life:—But in the Midst of all the Perplexity she was involv'd in, she now and then found a Mixture of Delight.—Ah! with what kind of Deceits does Love sometimes beguile the Imagination—What pleasing Chimera's does a Fancy, fired with that tender Flame, create!—What airy Prospects of unsubstantial Blessings present themselves to the deluded Eye, and cheat wile Though into an Extasy! *Anadea* had, in her Intervals of Pain, some of these Day-Dreams; she would sit and think that if the Chevalier *de Semar* should see a Woman whose superior Charms, or Fortune, should break off the Match, near as it was expected to be, or if some sudden Illness, or Accident, should take him from her by Death, how perfectly at liberty she then should be to indulge a more pleasing Passion for the lovely *Count*.—From this would she proceed farther, and think, that if thus free, there was a Possibility for him to regard her in an equal Tenderness, in what Manner she should behave, so as to secure his Heart.—Then would she form long Discourses, (such as 'tis probably he would indeed have made, had he been blest with an Opportunity,) and answer them again.—Nay, sometimes Contemplation, ravished with the rapturous Image, would carry her to a Confession of her Love; she yielded, fainted, almost died with Pleasure in the *Theory* of that Joy, the Practice of which she had ne'er experienced:—Then all at once, remembring it was but illusive, start from the fallacious Transport, and wake to real Woe and Bitterness of Heart.

But while she endured all this, and more than is in the Power of Language to express, she had her Revenge on the charming *Count* for the Inquietudes he had occasioned her, in as ample a Manner as she could have wished.—Being fully informed of the Truth of her Circumstances, by the Lady at whose House they had met, the Chagrin this Account gave him is scarce to be conceived:—The narrow Fortune he knew her Father was able to give her, was of itself sufficient to make him uneasy, for well he knew the Marquis designed him for more exalted Hopes, and would never consent he should marry a Woman, whose only Portion was her Wit and Beauty.—But, Love would have enabled him to get over that Difficulty: The history of her Engagement to the *Chevalier* was the distracting Point: He found immediately that his Passion would enable him to run all Risques for her sake, and dare all the Dangers which Disobedience might create, if in exchange for Grandeur, Wealth, and Favour, he could be possessed of her; but the Impossibility there appeared of gaining her, was near throwing him into Despair.—He knew that there was not many days before that fatal one arrived, which was to take from him the Power of even wishing to be hers, without being guilty of a Crime against her Honour, which he had too much Tenderness for her to suffer him to think of.—He knew not but her Affections might go hand-in-hand with her Duty in this marriage; but in case they did not, which he was willing to hope, yet the character he had heard of her Discretion and Modesty, made it difficult for him to flatter himself so far, as to believe she would, on any Consideration, incur the Censure of the Town, by breaking off with a Man to whom so publickly she was known to be engaged.—Thus for a while did the Suggestions of his Despair torment him: But these Agitations were not long thus violent; a Dawn of kinder Fortune at last broke out, and opened a more delightful Scene.—The Consideration of his Quality, his cast Estate, and some little Knowledge of his superior Perfections, seemed to console him with the Imagination that her Heart might not be so fixed in Tenderness to the *Chevalier*, but that such a Number of Advantages might loose the Chain.—Resolving to make the Experiment, he summoned all his Thought to assist him in the doing it:—He could not for a long Time decide, whether it were best to propose the Matter to the Father of *Anadea*, or herself: he knew very well, that old People are ambitious of their Children's Grandeur, and did not doubt but the Title he was able to confer on her, would weigh a great deal with him; but then he had heard so much of that Gentleman's Honour, and steddy Adherence to his Friend and Promise, that it deterred him; and, with Reason, believing that if he were refused there, he should never get an Opportunity of applying to the young Lady, he chose to make the first declaration to herself; the gaining her Affections being the material Point, he considered all others of little Consequence.—Having fixed his Determination he set himself down to frame a Letter to her; the Contents of which were in this Manner:

To the Divine ANADEA

Where the *Ill* is desperate, desperate *Remedies* are allow'd: Wanting the Glory of a long Train of Services to recommend my Passion, I should not dare, this unknown, unmeriting, to make a Declaration of the kind I am about to do, to the most excellent of her Sex, without being driven to it by an indispensible Necessity.—self-Preservation is the great Law of Nature: I can but die by your Disdain; and certain Death attends me, whenever you give the *Chevalier* a Blessing, which (if my good Genius had brought me to *Paris* timely enough to have given Proofs of a Passion which is not to be equall'd) you must, in Justice, have confess'd him less worthy of possessing.—I have seen you, have talk'd to you; O most adorable *Anadea!* have been a Witness of the Wonders of your Wit, and Beauty; and sure there needs no more to make a Soul, capable of distinguishing Perfection, feel for you all that Love inspires.—This is a Truth you must not know yourself to disbelieve.—'Tis easy for me to convince you I adore you; but, Oh! impossible to make you judge how much! That is a task, which the short Time allowed for my Probation, cannot accomplish.—Would any lucky Accident interpose, and for a while suspend my Rival's Happiness, I might, perhaps, do something should make you own I merit not your Scorn.— Injurious Fortune! And, O my Guardian Angel, too remissive of thy Charge! why had I not some secret Warnings of my

future Fate? why did I range so long in Foreign Courts, in search of trifling Pleasures, and unavailing Knowledge, while my eternal Ruin was at home contriving?—while all that could make me bless'd, was disposing to another?—But I grow wild! pardon the Frenzy which Despair occasions. My Death will soon be the Consequence of my Presumption, if you continue your cruel Resolution of giving yourself to *De Semar:* Then, 'tis possible, you will forgive and pity the
Unfortunate,
(But to the last Moment of his Life,)
the Adoring
De Blessure

P.S. Let your own Words pronounce my Doom, and I shall bless your Goodness.

To form any just Notion of what *Anadea* felt at the receipt of this Billet, one must be possessed of all those burning Passions with which the Sight of him who sent it had enflamed her Soul.—The utmost Extravagance of Joy and Surprise, at first invaded her; but sinking by degrees, gave way to Apprehensions, which to those who are acquainted with the Catastrophe of her unhappy Story, may be accounted Omens.—Though to be lov'd by *Blessure* was the highest Wish of her desiring Soul; though at the first Discovery that she was so, a Flood of Extasy ran thrilling through all her Veins, and each warm Fibre glow'd with immoderate Pleasure; yet Horror fill'd her Heart, a Terror, not to be accounted for, succeeded: Cold Tremblings seized her Limbs, her Eyes distilled unwilling Drops, and all the Opposites of Joy had a Vicissitude of equal Power.—Great part indeed of this might be thought to proceed from the Confusion she was in how to behave in an Exigence so dangerous either to her eternal Peace of Mind, or the Decorum of Duty and Modesty she had hitherto taken so much Care to preserve.—Though *Love* was a Passion she had but lately entertained, she found it grown too strong for Controul; and *Reserve*, though long habitual to her, now difficult to be maintained.—How hard was it to resolve what Course to take? She must determine either to do the extremest Violence to her Inclinations, or forfeit all Title to a Character she esteem'd equal to her Life.—Ah! how dreadful is the Conflict, when Love and Honour rack the divided Soul?—How small the Relief we can receive from Reason?—Poor *Anadea*, though by Strength of Mind, more than most of her Sex enabled to endure it, could not for a long Time get through this Dilemma, and the Messenger who brought the Cause of it, was obliged to remind her three or four Times that he waited for an Answer, before she could enough submit to the Suggestions of either her Passion, or Prudence, to be able to make one. But when she did, it was as follows:

To Count BLESSURE

My Lord,

    Though a Maid in my Circumstances might very well be excused returning any Answer to a Letter of that Nature I have received from your Lordship, yet I chuse rather to incur the Censure of *Indiscreet,* than *Ungrateful!*; which latter I must be, if I did not acknowledge the Obligation your too good Opinion of my little Merit has conferred on me; and since by those who have the Disposal of me, I am deprived of everything to pay you back but Thanks, intreat you will accept of them, when offered in the sincerest Manner, by,

My Lord,
Your Lordship's,
Most humble Servant,
ANADEA

The Force she put on herself in writing in this Manner, when she would have given almost her Life to have pour'd out the tender over-powering Languishments, that took up all her Soul, may justly make her an Object of Admiration:—It would be endless to represent the various Turns of disorder'd Emotions which run through her troubled Mind after the Departure of the Messenger.—Sometimes she wished a second Sollicitation;—at others she trembled, for fear she should again be put to so severe a Trial, which she could not promise herself to go through with the same Fortitude and Resolution as before.—However, I believe most Women will imagine she would have thought it a greater Misfortune, had the *Count* here ceased his Prosecution, than all she could sustain from the Continuance of it: But he was not a Lover so easily repulsed; he found in that little Note great Matter of Consolation;—he interpreted her telling him, *Since deprived by those who had the Power over her, from everything but Thanks*, that her consenting to a Marriage with the Chevalier *De Semar*, was the Effect only of that Duty she owed her Father, and that her own Inclination had nothing to do in that Affair; for if it had (said he to himself) she would have added, *by my own Choice, as well as the Power of those who have the Disposal of me.*—This Imagination emboldened him to write immediately; and before she was certain whether she really desired he should, or not, she received by the same Hand which brought the other, this second Billet.

To the Too-charming and most Adorable
ANADEA

The Trouble you have given yourself, divinest *Anadea!* is a Favour which the unhappy *Blessure* can never sufficiently acknowledge. I own your Goodness not inferior to you other unmatched Charms: Oh! were you half so sensible, as you ought, of that Heaven of Perfections you are Mistress of, you would not thus rashly, thus hastily resign it!—You would at least defer giving my rival that Profusion of Happiness, which though no Man can be said to deserve, yet some may boast a more justifiable Plea than what proceeds meerly from the ingratiating himself to the Favour of others.—'Tis your own Inclinations only that ought to have the Power of disposing you; and if they speak not in his Favour, O let me conjure you, for your own sake, for the sake of your eternal Peace, not to offer a Violation to those sacred Dictates.—If the Wretch, who presumes to give you this Advice, has not the Power of pleasing, that Softness in your Eyes and Form shews you were not born to be forever unsusceptible of the Force of Love; and though you ne'er can find an Object worthy of inspiring it, you may hereafter find one to whom your Liking may give a Lustre; and then, how truly unfortunate would you be?—O consider it aright!—Delay a while these Nuptials!—Think 'tis your good Genius warns you!—A little time, perhaps, may make you know I have not counselled Ill!—But whither does my Zeal transport me?—I have declared myself too far interested in this Cause, not to render everything I urge suspected.—But, by Heaven! by that

Heaven which gave you that Transcendency of Charms, and me of Adoration! were I perfectly assur'd, of what I fear, that all that I can do, or all I would do, had I the Power, would never influence your Soul in pity of my Passion, then I would plead as now:—O let *Hymen* wait, till *Love,* soft *Love,* shall introduce him!—But you, perhaps, will say that 'tis already done in favour of the Chevalier.—If so, I have indeed nothing to object, but what may justly be imputed to a too partial Wish for my own Happiness, and Envy of another's.—Silence me then at once; confess your Passion for this fortunate, this triumphant Man! and end the Boldness, the Sufferings which occasioned it, and the Life of him, who without *Anadea,* thinks Death a Blessing.

Your Everlasting Votary,
Blessure

Anadea now perceived whence he had drawn his Encouragement to write again, but was not so much displeased at it, as she would have perswaded herself she was: And her Duty every Moment growing weaker, as her Passion stronger, she with much less Reluctance that she had felt in answering the former, sent him a Reply in these Words:

To Count Blessure

My Lord,

 I am so little accustomed to a Correspondence of this Nature, that 'tis not to be wondered at that I should lay myself open to many Disadvantages:—But as much a stranger as I am to Gallantry, I am yet a much greater to Dissimulation; and though it may be the most prudent to pretend I have given my *Heart* where I shortly must my *Hand,* yet I cannot forbear confessing, with that Freedom you require, that it is to the *Chevalier's* future Behaviour he must owe that Part of me.—The rest my Father has an indisputable Right to dispose of, as he thinks fit; and however averse my Inclinations may be, Obedience, as it is sometimes the severest, is sure the most valuable Part of a Child's Duty; and this Task I shall always enjoin myself. If I find any Difficulties in the Performance, the greater Glory will it be to conquer them: And it is by such Proofs of Virtue alone, that I can hope to merit any of those Praises, you have so profusely lavished on me, and for which I must ever acknowledge myself,

My Lord,

Your Lordship's

Most Oblig'd,

ANADEA

It was with an Infinity of Transport that the Count received this Assurance from her own Hand, that her intended Marriage with the *Chevalier* was not the Effect of her Choice.—his Joy had been immoderate, had not the latter part of her Letter, wherein she expresses so strict a Resolution to follow Duty, something abated it.—He did not absolutely despair, however; and knowing he had no Time to lose, early the next Morning a Messenger from him saluted her with these Lines:

To the Forever ador'd ANADEA

Can you then, O more than Angel, at the Expence of your whole Life's Peace, resolve to bless the Man, who has it not in his Power to return one Grain of Joy, for that exhaustless Store he must forever find in the Possession of your Charms? Can you be so severely just to *Duty*, yet so relentless to the Calls of *Love*?—How small was the Request I made, and that too not for my own, but your infinitely to me more valuable sake, that you would, for a Time, a little Time, suspend the cruel Bliss designed him?—But you think it a Virtue to grant him all, while you refuse me everything!—I will not, however, desist from my Sollicitations, and though I have but little Encouragement to hope you will allow me that Liberty, intreat you will permit my *Tongue* to attempt that which my *Pen* has been unable to perform.—I beg you will allow me once to throw myself beneath you Feet, and if all I can then urge is ineffectual to move your Soul, will never ask it more.—Yes, most adorable *Anadea!* I will then take my everlasting Farewel of those Eyes, those amiable Eyes, whose sweet Enchantments, in a Moment do the Work of Ages, and shed an Influence never, never to be eraz'd.—If my Presence will be an Offence to him whom you are so willing to oblige, my Visit shall be Private, or if you please, will attend you at the House of that Lady, where I had the Glory (for so I still will call it) of becoming your Slave, and receiving those Wounds, which soon you'll find too fatal not to merit your Compassion.—If I am not hated by you,—if the Presumption of my Love declar'd be not a Crime beyond Forgiveness, deny not this last Request to him, whom your Cruelty will shortly render unable to make more:—Though, if there be Remembrance in the Grave, your Prosperity and Happiness shall be the endless Wish of

The Undone
BLESSURE

What now became of the enamour'd *Anadea*? How was it possible for a Heart so prepossessed as her's, to hold out in a Reserve which was very near breaking the Strings which held it.—Through Fire, through all the Dangers that Imagination can invent, would she have flown, once more to have seen the ador'd Object of her Affections: How then could she deny herself that Happiness, when pressed to it by him with such Tenderness? Yet still the Consequences that might attend this Meeting, for a Time repelled the Dictates of her Passion.—But it was no more than a faint Struggle; Love! all-conquering, all-o'er-powering Love! triumphed over every other Consideration! and she consented to his and her own impatient Wishes, in these Words:

To Count BLESSURE

My Lord,

The Concern you are pleased still to express for my Peace of Mind, is too obliging not to commend my utmost Esteem: I cannot, without being guilty of ill Manners to you, and Unkindness to myself, refuse the Honour you would do me of a Visit; but because it may raise a Suspicion, which I would avoid, chuse rather to wait your coming at that Lady's you mention. A Conversation such as yours is too improving, too agreeable, not to be accepted with the highest Satisfaction; and you extremely wrong me, if you think I look on it as any other than the Effect of my ill

Fortune, that I have it not in my Power to give you greater Proofs of Friendship than the Grant of this Request; which tho' it may seem of little Consequence, might be dangerous, if the Justice of my Reasons were not sufficient to bear down the Sophistry of all those you are prepar'd to give me, in Prejudice of that Duty I have sworn to maintain while I am,

ANADEA

P.S. I will be this Evening about Five at the appointed Place.

The *Count*, as he had good Cause, now thought he had gained his Point: He examined all her Letters again and again, and found not one Word in any of them which seemed to express a Dislike of him, and in this last very much on the contrary; and though he was free from Vanity, could not forbear indulging himself with the Reflection, that it must be more than an ordinary Esteem and bare Civility which could influence a Woman of *Anadea's* reserved Temper to act in the Manner she did: And beginning to hope her Heart was of his Party, did not much doubt but he should find Arguments to confute all those that Duty could raise in Opposition to his Wishes.

Full of Impatience, and some Mixture of Fears and Doubts, which yet were infinitely greater on her Side than his, did both wait the expected Hour; which being arrived, they happened to go so exactly at the Hour, that they met each other at the Door. Madamoiselle *De Flores* (for so was that Lady call'd) happening to be abroad, the Count, unwilling to lost the Opportunity, took the Liberty of entreating her to walk into the *Tuilleries* with him; which, she having gone this Length, made no Scruple of obliging him in. The Count in secret bless'd his good Start, which had favour'd him with an Advantage he could not have hop'd for in that Lady's House; for she being of a Coquette humour, and beside, not in the least appris'd of the Reasons of their coming, would have given him very little Time to entertain his ador'd *Anadea* in the Manner he desir'd; nor was she, whose Guesses were the same with his, much less satisfy'd with the Accident. It not being the Time of the Day in which Company usually walk, made the Place they were in extremely retir'd, and they had the good Fortune of meeting no Interruption.—I believe it would be but needless to inform the Reader what kind of Conversation it was with which these two amiable Persons entertain'd each other: By what has been already said of the Violence of that Passion which influenc'd both their Souls, 'tis easy to imagine nothing was omitted on his Side that Love could inspire, or Eloquence find Words for; and that she having made this Condescension not out of a womanish Pride, or Fondness of hearing fine Things said to her, but purely oblig'd to it by the Force of an Inclination too powerful to be resisted, could not now restrain those soft Emotions which had brought her thither with so much Artifice, but that he discover'd enough to make him happy.— That Passion is but weak which stands in need of the Language of the Tongue to make itself believ'd:—A thousand Ways it speaks; each Look, each little Motion will betray it:—In vain we wear the Mask of cold Indifference;—in vain affect Reserve and formal Distance: The intestine Flame breaks out the more, the more we would conceal it, bursts out in Sighs, and blazes in our Glances.—In spite of *Anadea's* Efforts to the contrary, the lovely Count read in her sparkling Eyes the long'd-for Secret, perceived the soft Desire flow on her blushing Cheeks, and tremble in her faultering Accents.—Wrapp'd in a Joy too violent for Constraint, it was not in his Power to hide the mighty Transport:—He flew upon her, caught her in his Arms, and half smothering her with eager Kisses, which he ravish'd from her Lips and Breast, soon let her know her Cautions had been fruitless; that he was conscious of the Blessing he possess'd, and triumph'd over the *Chevalier* in the noblest Part of her, her Soul. But with what Words is there a Possibility of representing the Shame, the Confusion of *Anadea*, at a Behaviour so different from that which she expected, and so much alter'd from that humble Awe with which he had at first approach'd her; but assuming, as much as she could, an Air of Resentment, she reproach'd the unliscens'd Liberty he had taken, in Terms as severe as her Heart would give her Leave to do; but though not altogether so harsh as would have proceeded from a Person to whom he was indifferent, yet they were such as would have very much confounded him, if all the Time she was speaking them, the same tender Symptoms already mention'd, had not assur'd him the Offence he had been guilty of was not too great to be forgiven.—He entreated her Pardon, however, in Expressions as full of Humility as the most haughty of her Sex could wish, and reiterated numberless Protestations, that encourag'd Hope should never transport him to transgress the Rules of Honour; and happening to say that he would not, even in a Wish, violate that Respect which was his Duty to pay her, she instantly catch'd at that Word, and interrupting him; No more (said she) shall all the Perfections you are Master of oblige me to neglect that which I ought to pay to him that gave me Being:—And whatever I may suffer by it, will find some Pretence to hasten the Performance to the *Chevalier*, lest hereafter it should not be in my Power to do it.—She utter'd this with so much seeming Courage, that the Extasy with which the *Count* has so lately been taken up, was not a little abated:—But, alas! what are the Resolutions of a *Lover*? The smallest Gale of tender Sighs from the believed Object puffs them away, they mix with the Air, and are no more remember'd.—They parted not till he had prevailed on her not only to recede from that cruel Determination of hast'ning the intended Marriage, but also, instead of that, to do her utmost Endeavours to delay it, and in the mean Time, continue a Correspondence with him by Letters, or otherways, according as Opportunity, and his Invention to find some Stratagem to procure him that Happiness, should permit her to allow it.

When once a Mind truly fir'd by *Love* is in pursuit of the Gratification of its Wishes, no Reflections have the Force to put a stop to the Career, to damp the Joy of Hope, or quell the Anxieties of Doubt. The *Count*, transported with the Progress he had made on the Affections of *Anadea*, thought of nothing but how he should increase the Tenderness he found she had for him, and raise it to a Pitch unable to deny him anything: Nor had he any Reason to despair that, having obtained so far of her as to suspend the Marriage with his Rival, he should in a little Time prevail on her to put him in his Place, and gave himself up wholly to Joy. In what Manner the *Marquis* his father would receive her as a Daughter, or how he would look on himself for having made a Choice so far beneath what he designed for him, and without his Knowledge or Consent; all this never came into his Thoughts, or if it did, it vanished like a vapour: Bless'd in his *Love,* he seem'd but little to regard the rest, and left the Event to Fortune to determine.

But it was not in this Manner the poor *Anadea* made herself Reparation for the Inquietudes she had sustain'd: She was now fill'd with more and greater than before; not that her Passion would not have enabled her endure as much as his could do, and left her as little the Power of Consideration for herself.—Disobedience to her Father, and Breach of the Promise she had made to the *Chevalier*, were Crimes which grew less and less formidable: She could have been contented to have suffer'd any Reproach, any Shame, any Punishment for *Blessure*; but the Apprehensions of making him unfortunate, was the severest Dagger to her Soul.—She foresaw a Train of Ills, the Consequences of being his Wife; yet, but what she believed of *his* passion, and was certain of her *own*, though to become so, was unavoidable, without an imminent Hazard of Death of Distraction to them both.—Thus did she afflict herself; and the inward Agonies of her Mind immediately wrought such an Alteration in her Looks, that feigning herself Sick (which was the only Pretence she could find out for delaying the Marriage with *De Semar*) none suspected it for any other than real.

It is hard to say whether her Father or the *Chevalier* was most concerned for her imagined Indisposition, both loved her with an equal Tenderness, though in a different Manner; and she receiv'd so many Instances in that Time of this young Gentleman's Good Nature and Affection, that it very much added to her other Perturbations, that she was forc'd by a more prevailing Passion to deceive him.

A Physician was sent for to attend the fair Patient; but the *Count* being apprised of his Name by *Anadea*, for that Purpose, by a private Billet, he made him a Visit, and a Present too considerable, not to make the Person who received it wholly devoted to his Interest.—After feeling her Pulse, and the usual Formalities on those Occasions, he told the old Gentleman and intended Bridegroom, who were impatiently waiting his Opinion, that the Lady was at present extremely Ill; and that he fear'd all he could prescribe for her Recovery would be of little Service without Change of Air.—It was therefore wholly necessary for her Recovery, that she should be removed, and advised to have her carry'd toward *Versailles*, which he told them was a most excellent Situation, and the the Recipe's he should apply, he hoped to work a perfect Cure of the malady she at present labour'd under.

The Doctor having done his Part, *Anadea* failed not in hers, and reminded her Father, that she had an intimate Friend who had a Country Seat near *Versailles*; and that she was certain not only of a Welcome there, but also of being taken greater Care of then she could expect from a Stranger.—The indulgent Parent heard the Proposal with Satisfaction, and everything was ordered to be got ready for her Removal with all Expedition. She was carried in a *Litter* for Ease, and the assiduous *Chevalier* attended her on Horseback to the Place she was to go, which being so small a Distance from *Paris*, made him the more consoled at leaving her, because he could with Ease make her a Visit everyday. Unhappy Gentleman! he little thought how little welcome he was grown, and that he had left her in a Place where the Person who had supplanted him, would have the Opportunity of being with her every Hour.

It was to the House of Madamoiselle *De Flores* that the Counterfeit Indispos'd was carry'd; and the *Count*, who had put this Stratagem into *Anadea's* Head, was lodged next Door. Had he thought for to have entrusted that Lady with the Affair, or his going into that Part of the Country, she would doubtless have made him an Offer of being under the same Roof with his Mistress; but he considered her as a Woman not to be depended on in a Case such as this, and she knew no more than what was publickly believ'd, that *Anadea* being really very Ill, was advised to that Place, for the Benefit of the Air; and not being of a temper to love Retirement, made an Excuse, (which was received better than she imagined) that having some great Business in Town, it was impossible for her to be at *Versailles* herself. The Lovers by this Means had all the Opportunity imaginable of entertaining one another. The *Count* was scarce ever from her, and pretending to the Servants of Madamoiselle *De Flores*, that he was a Person who the Physicians had appointed to attend her, was not at all suspected for any other than what he seemed. Thus it went on for several Days; but the impatient *Blessure* putting her in mind that it would be impossible to carry on the Deceit much longer, and that then she would be forced to the Arms of the *Chevalier*, at last won her to consent to end his Fears, by yielding to be his Wife.—This Grant obtained, he easily found Means to get a Priest into the House, who for a Fee, like that he gave the Physician, tied the indissoluble Knot, and with as little Difficulty concealed himself in her Chamber, and when all the Family were hush'd, and there remained no Danger of Interruption, consummated that Felicity he so ardently had languish'd for—She was now his own; and she who was hardly brought to make a Breach in her Duty to a Parent, would not be guilty of a Sin against it to her Husband: He demanded the full Possession of her Charms the next Night, and the next after that, and so on; and she was too obedient to refuse, in spite of the Risque of a Discovery, which by such repeated Ventures might possibly fall our, to the Destruction of that Scheme they had laid and agreed to follow, never to reveal their Marriage till the Death of the Marquis *De Blessure*. The *Bride*, however, was not without her Fears, and in midst of all those Raptures which attend reciprocal Affection, rais'd to be the most elevated Height that human Nature can sustain, she would on a sudden start, and imagine she heard somebody in the Room, or listening at the Door.—Nor did her Apprehensions deceive her: An old Maid, who was a sort of Governante over the rest of the Servants, happening to sit up latter than ordinary, fancy'd she heard something like the Murmurs of a Voice in *Anadea's* Chamber, which unfortunately was directly under that in which she was: She had before some little Suspicion on the too constant Attendance which the *Count* paid his suppos'd *Patient*, and easily perceiving that of whatever sort her Distemper was, it was not dangerous enough to require a Physician always present, was resolved to be satisfy'd of the Truth.—She stole softly down Stairs, and was perfectly convinc'd there was somebody in the Room beside *Anadea*, because she heard two Voices, tho' she could not distinguish what they said—She kept close Watch, however, went not to Bed all Night, and early in the Morning saw him go out at a little back Gate which opened into the Fields, and shut it softly after him, as was his Custom, before any of the Family were stirring.—This Creature, who had a greater share of *Honesty* than *Good Nature*, and was more *scrupulous* than *wise*, thought Concealment of an Affair, such as she fancied that was, a Sin, and immediately write her Lady an Account of all she had discovered.—Madamoiselle *De Flores*, though she was no Enemy to Intrigue, could not forgive it in a Person who made not choice of her for a Confidante, and failed not to whisper it in all Company she came into! The Report spread so far (as Scandal is always industrious) that it came to the Ears of some of the *Chevalier's* nearest Friends and Relations, who being not very well pleas'd at his marrying without a Fortune, were glad of this Occasion to express their Dislike.—They acquainted him with what had been told them, with all the aggravating Circumstances imaginable: But his good opinion of *Anadea's* Virtue was too deeply rooted for this Aspersion to remove:—He was so far from giving Credit to it, that he protested, whoever endeavoured to impose on his Belief in that Manner he would look on as his mortal Enemy, and avoid as he would Hell.—It had, perhaps, rested here, if one of the Persons who were his Informers had not added, that he had it from the Mouth of the Madamoiselle *De Flores*, to whose House his imaginary virtuous Lady had retired, under pretence of Sickness, but in reality to meet her Gallant with greater Privacy.—This so nettled him, that he went that Moment to wait on that Lady; not that he yet believ'd the Accusation, or that she had reported it, but to oblige her to confute a Falsehood, of which she was said to be the Author.—But with what Words can I set forth the Confusion of this surpris'd astonish'd Lover, when he heard her frankly own all he had been told, for Truth, and was by her shewed the Letter which her Maid had writ?—He stamp'd about the Room, tore his Hair, rav'd like one distracted, knew not what to think,—nor how to proceed to find the fatal Certainty of what he now began to fear.—At last (for what is so ingenious as Female Malice in Invention!) she told him she would put him in a Way to prove the Dishonour of her whom he esteemed so virtuous.—I dare so much rely (*said she*) on the Integrity of my Servant, that I will write a Letter to her, of which, if you think fit, you shall yourself, in some Disguise, be Bearer: She shall conceal you in the House, till you have an Opportunity of making your own Eyes the Witnesses of what she has alledged. The *Chevalier* extremely approv'd of this Advice, but as to the Disguise, told her it needed not; for it being customary for him to go thither everyday, it was but his tarrying there, after he had taken Leave, and watching the Approach of this happy Favourite.—That is true, indeed, (replied the Lady;) I had forgot:—But I would caution you not to take the least Notice of this to the old Gentleman, who, though a perfect honest Man, may do much to save a Daughter's Character.—He will certainly send to apprise her of it, and make her on her Guard.—To convince you that I will not (resum'd the *Chevalier*) I will not leave your House till I take Horse for *Versailles*; If you please, therefore, to prepare my Credential to your Maid, my Servant in the mean Time shall get my Horses ready.—Every Thing being thus agreed on, she immediately went to her Closet, and writ these Lines, which she read to him before she seal'd it.

To Flavilla

It lies on you to prove the Truth of what you write
concerning *Anadea*.—This Gentleman is dubious of it.—
Conceal him in the House, unknown to any of the Family,
till you find an Opportunity of convincing him by Ocular
Demonstrations.—Neglect it not, if you would escape the
Punishment due to Traducers, or preserve a Friend of your
Mistress.

De Lores

This was writ in a Manner so assur'd and certain, that he almost doubted whether he need seek a farther Confirmation; but the Charms of *Anadea* raising in his Soul a Flood of Tenderness, told him he ought to have the utmost Proof e'er he believ'd her guilty; and away he went towards *Versailles*, with Agitations which never had accompany'd him before: But when he arriv'd there, and came into the Presence of *Anadea*, how hard it was for him to retain those Suspicions Madamoiselle *De Flores* had inspir'd him with; but resolving on the promis'd Proof, he made a short Visit, and shewing the Letter to the Servant, and examining her on the Occasion, grew more fearful than before, that he should find all he had been told too just. The informing Servant, as it behov'd her, was not doubly diligent in her Watch; she saw the Person enter, and took Care the Family should go to Bed betimes, that he might venture to stay with the more Security:—And everything being order'd proper for the Design, it had the Effect she both expected and wish'd;—and in the Dead of the Night, when the endearing Pair thought themselves most happy, most secure, they were on a sudden surpris'd with Shrieks, and a great Cry of Thieves. The watchful Spy began it, and in a Moment the frighted Servants took the Alarm, started from their Beds, and echo'd round the House the Noise:—Here, (said she, running towards the Chamber of *Anadea*,) here the Villains broke it:—Where, where? cry'd one.—How many are they? bawl'd out another:—Ring the Bell, said a Third:—Who shall venture to the Turret? rejoin'd a different Voice:— All was in an Uproar, everyone in Confusion.—The *Count*, equally distracted between the Care of preserving *Anadea's* Person, and her Honour, knew not what was best to do in this Extremity; but jumping out of the Bed on the first Beginning of the Noise, made a shift to get some Part of his Cloaths on, before, under pretence of searching for the Ruffians, they burst the Door open.—The Lights which some of them had in their Hands, gave to the amaz'd *Chevalier* not only a Confirmation of his Misfortune, but the Knowledge of his *Rival*: He had frequently seen *Blessure*; and though the Habit he was then in was plain, and far different from what he wore when he appear'd himself, yet the Features of his Face could not be disguis'd from him who ever had been Witness of their uncommon Beauty.—But in this Discovery he had the Advantage of him; for the *Count* thinking no other than that there were really Thieves in the House, cry'd out to them to be gone, and not fright the Lady; if there were Ruffians, he would join with them in the Search.—None but what is in this Room, (interrupted fiercely the *Chevalier*:) You are the Villain we pursue; and hadst thou ten thousand Lives, they all should perish in this Expiation of that Lady's Honour.—He had not finish'd those Words, when *Anadea* giving a great Shriek, cry'd out, Ah, we are betray'd! Guard,—guard your Life, my Lord!—How! Is it so? (resum'd *Blessure*.) Thus, then, I retort the Villain back to him that gave it.—There was no farther Room for Speech; the Fury with which both were possess'd, left neither of them the Power of making that Use of their Weapons which is taught in School, and running at each other with equal Violence, both of them receiv'd Wounds, which either of them would have had Skill to parry, had the Cause for which they fought been of less Consequence.—But that which the *Count* gave to the *Chevalier*, took away all occasion for a second; the unhappy Gentleman instantly fell dead on the Place.—And all this was over in so short a Time, that the Servants, confounded and unable to guess the Meaning of what they saw, had not the means of preventing it, thought they had of securing the *Count*, but the Orders of that directing Wench, whose Officiousness had been the Cause of this Scene of Woe.

What was now the Horror, the Distraction of *Anadea*! scarce could they, who had compassionate Souls enough to endeavour it, keep Life in her.—She saw the Man, who by her Father's Command, and her own solemn Promise, ought to have been her Husband, lie dead before her;—kill'd by him whom her inconsiderate Passion had led her to marry, in spite of Duty or Pre-engagement.—But that, though terrible, was not the greatest and most shocking Part of her Calamity:—Her dear *Blessure*, her ador'd, adoring Bridegroom, was torn from her; she knew not well whither, or if not near the same Condition to which he had reduc'd his Rival.—She saw him hurt,—she beheld his precious Blood spilt for her sake, and was deny'd the Privilege of binding up his Wounds,—of seeing him, or consulting what was best to be done for their common interest or Safety.—But when Morning came, she was eas'd of some Part of the Dilemma she was in; one of the Servants told her that Horses being got ready, she must prepare to attend to *Paris* the body of the *Chevalier*, with that Gentleman, (for as yet they knew not who the *Count* was,) who had so cruelly murder'd him, there to give an Account of their Actions, and by what Means this Misfortune was brought about.—To hear that her dear Lord was not so dangerously wounded as her Fears for him had suggested, gave an inexpressible Alleviation to the Torments she had endur'd; and though there were yet many remaining Reasons of Disquiet, she supported them with a Fortitude, which till them she knew not herself was Mistress of.— What most try'd her Patience, was, that during the Time of their little Journey, she could not be admitted to speak to the *Count*, who being bound and pinion'd, was put into the Litter with the dead Body of the *Chevalier*; and she mounted behind one of the Servants, was oblig'd to ride, encompass'd by a Crowd of People, who seem'd a Guard about her, at a good Distance from the Treasure of her Soul.

At their Arrival in *Paris*, the *Count* was immediately known; and the Discovery of his Quality made those to whose Custody he was deliver'd, oblig'd to use him with more Civility than those Rusticks had done, who before had the Charge of him. However, the fact being plainly proved upon him by a great Number of Witnesses, he was, by the Magistrates apply'd to for that Purpose, committed to close confinement.—*Anadea*, though carry'd to no other Place than her Father's House, was not more at Liberty; all was now discover'd; her Dislike of the *Chevalier*, her pretended Indisposition to avoid marrying him, her Passion for the *Count*, every Particular of the Transaction by this Account laid open.—Nothing was a Secret, but that she was his Wife; and that, no Reproaches, no Shame, no Terrors, could draw from her; not doubting, but if that were known, it would incense the *Marquis* and others of his Relations so far against him, that they would take but little Care to defend him from the Prosecutions the Friends of the *Chevalier* would make against him.

Blessure, in the mean time, was not idle in his Imprisonment; having obtain'd his dear *Anadea*, he thought Life, and the Possession of her, a Blessing too great to part with, if by any Means to be preserv'd.—He neglected nothing therefore that might be of Service to him; and the extraordinary Qualifications he was Master of, join'd to the sweetest and most affable Disposition in the World, had rais'd him so many Friends, that, with the Interest his Father had with the King, gave him great hopes of a Pardon.—The old *Marquis*, as 'tis not to be thought otherwise, came from his *Villa* immediately to *Paris*, on the first News of this Misfortune, and left no Means untry'd to save his only and beloved Son; but all his Sollicitations promis'd him but little Success, and he was ready to fall into Despair, when he was sent for by Madam *De la Roche*. This Lady was at that Time one of the King's most favourite Mistresses: She had a Daughter, on whose Heart the Charms of the young *Blessure* had made the most sensible Impression; which being discover'd by her Mother, who tenderly loved her, she doubted not but the *Marquis* would think a Pardon for his Son a sufficient Dower, if there had been no other Motives to induce his Consent to the Match; but withal, she was not only a great Fortune, but also a celebrated Beauty. It was with an inexpressible Joy the old *Marquis* listen'd to the Proposal; and promised for his Son everything they desir'd. In fine, all being agreed on, Madam *De la Roche* went immediately to the King, threw herself at his Feet, and intreated this Proof of his Affection with so much Zeal and Tenderness, that she succeeded; and before the *Marquis*, who had staid sometime to entertain his design'd Daughter-in Law, had left her House, return'd with the so-much-despair'd-of Pardon in her Hand.—The Transport of a Father for the Life of an only Child, may better be imagin'd than express'd; and after making those Retributions to the Lady which such an Obligation demanded, it was concluded among them, that they should go all together to the *Bastile*, and overjoy him with the News of Life, and Liberty restor'd, who by this Time began to think of nothing less.—The Sight of these two Ladies, one of whose Sentiments he was not unacquainted with, gave him some little Suspicion of the Truth; and he receiv'd the Congratulations they made him on his Pardon with a Coldness which surpris'd everybody, because he doubted not but there was a Price requir'd for it, which he was utterly unable to pay.—It was not long before he was confirm'd in this Conjecture, his Father taking young Madam *De la Roche* by the Hand, and presenting her to him, it is not (*said he*) for your Life alone that you are indebted to this Lady, but for a much greater Blessing, her Love: Through all the Disadvantages of that Character your criminal Acquaintance with *Anadea* has drawn on you, she finds something in you to approve:—'Tis your Part therefore to endeavour to deserve her Goodness, and by your future Behaviour expiate the past. Though from the first Moment of their Appearance, the *Count* had expected a Salutation of this Nature, the Mention of *Anadea* with Dishonour, gave him a Shock he was not arm'd against.—He redden'd extremely, and with a Voice which express'd the utmost Discontent,—If, my Lord, (*reply'd he,*) you would have me think the Tidings you bring essential to my Happiness, you will not name that Lady in the Affair, which, if truly reported, would not be to the Disadvantage of her Fame.—How! (*interrupted the* Marquis, *fiercely*) not to the Disadvantage of her Fame? Were there not a Train of Evidences to prove her Fault?—Did not all the Family of Madamoiselle *De Flores* depose the shameful Truth?—Is not the whole World appris'd of it?—If it were so (*resum'd the* Count, *with equal Warmth,*) if all they have sworn were just, the Blame ought to be mine;—but People often judge by Appearances:—This Affair may not be what it seems.—

The Dispute had rose much higher than it did, if Madam *De la Roche* had not moderated the *Marquis's* growing Indignation, by telling him, he ought not to take ill the Concern his Son express'd, since it was rather a Proof of Honour to vindicate that of a Lady who lov'd him, than the contrary; and that if he would oblige her, he should mention it no more.—You see, (*resum'd he,*) the Obligations you have to the Goodness of this Lady; and I hope you will give a Proof of that Honour you seem to stand so much upon, by studying to be grateful.—I am indeed (*answer'd the* Count, *gloomily*) indebted past Power of returning, but shall endeavour it.—You must, (*interrupted his Father.*) In what I can, I will, my Lord, (*rejoined the other.*) With these Words, the *Marquis* taking Madam *De la Roche* by the hand, oblig'd the *Count* to do the same by the Daughter, and they all went into the Coach, the *Marquis* having discharg'd the necessary Fees for the Prisoner's leaving the *Bastile* as he came up.

It was the Coach was order'd to drive; where he was soon made acquainted with the History of the Misfortune he fear'd.—The *Marquis*, after relating at full the Obligations he had to that Lady, told him what he had promis'd in his name, and that he must Resolve in a very few Days to make her his Wife.—The perplexity the *Count* was in, in what Manner he should reply, depriv'd him, for some Moments, of the Power of doing it; which Hesitation inflaming the arbitrary Nature of the passionate Marquis: And is the Command I give you (said he,) such as can possibly occasion a Demur, whether you should obey, or not?—If not all this Lady's Charms have Force to influence you, to accept her as the choicest Gift of Heaven; if all she has done for you is not enough to excite your Gratitude, you are not now to be told, that my *Will* is of itself sufficient to force you to Compliance.—Not to an impossibility, as this perhaps may be, (replied the *Count:*) But, however, (continu'd he, bowing with all Humility,) nothing can make me so truly miserable, as being constrain'd to appear guilty of a Failure in that Duty I owe your Lordship, or Ingratitude to Persons I am so highly oblig'd to, as I am to these Ladies.—I beg, therefore, a short Time for Consideration.—This Evening I will attend you at your Lodgings, and endeavour to prove myself obedient. With these Words he went out of the Room. But as the *Marquis* was rising from his Chair, more enraged than before, with an Intention to stop him, Madam *De la Roche*, tho' but little satisfied with his Behaviour in reality, seem'd to excuse it, and told him, that she did not in the least question, but when he reflected on the Advantages there were in a Marriage with her Daughter, he would readily enough assent to the Proposal; and entreated he would be calm, at least, till he heard his Answer.—The young Lady could not so well conceal her Resentment; her Blushes, and the Sighs which issued from her Breast, in spite of her Efforts to the contrary, disclos'd it plain.—All this little Company had their Share of Disquiets, and utterly unable to say anything which might be of Comfort to each other, broke up much sooner than they design'd.—The Ladies remain'd at home to indulge their several Discontents, and the *Marquis* retir'd to his Lodgings, to wait the coming of his Son. But that young Gentleman had a Distress of Soul which his Father, unknowing of his Reasons, and also of a Nature not very tender, was far from conceiving.—The Moment he left the House of Madam *De la Roche*, he went to *Anadea*, whom he had never seen since the fatal Night of his being surpris'd with her in the Manner already represented, and whom he now found in a Confusion, and Depth of Sorrow, which heighten'd his own.—The Reader will easily believe, this unhappy Lady had endur'd all that can be imagin'd of soul-rending Reproaches, which a Father could utter in the Distraction of Thought for the imagin'd Dishonour of a belov'd Child: But all she knew he felt, could not prevail on her to reveal what she believ'd might be prejudicial to her dear *Blessure*.—In fine, the Sense of these Misfortunes struck so deep an Impression on the Mind of this Gentleman, who valued the Honour of his Family above his Life, that in a few Days he broke his Heart: But not even to see him in the Agonies of death could prevail on her to disclose the Secret, and he left the World with an Opinion of her Guilt;—It was not an Hour after he was no more, that she was told Count *Blessure* was come to visit her. The Surprise, the Extasy of Joy which seiz'd her Spirit, at hearing he was at Liberty, immediately succeeding as excessive a one of Grief, was very near throwing her into the same Condition with her Father: She swoon'd at Sight of him, and when she recover'd, had not for sometime the Power of Speech: But what her Tongne denied, her Arms made Reparation for.—She fell on his Neck, and grasp'd him with convulsive Strainings which made him fear their Violence would be fatal.

When the first Emotions of their mutual Transport would admit of cooler Conversations, he recounted to her all that had passed since the Time of their Separation: But when he came to that Part which made mention of Madam *De la Roche*, she discover'd so visible a Disorder, that he was oblig'd to give over the Discourse, and reassure her with ten thousand Endearments, and Vows of an eternal Fidelity, before he could restore the faded Colour to her Cheeks. After a long Consultation what was best to be done, it was at last agreed, still to preserve the Secret of their Marriage, and that he should lay the Blame of his refusing the Proposal made by Madam *De la Roche* on want of Inclination, rather than a Pre-engagement.—The one, he thought, might gain him Time; but a Confession of the other seem'd to promise nothing but immediate Ruin.— He knew his father's avaricious Disposition too well, to imagine he would ever consent to espousing any Woman, who had not a Fortune equal to his own, much less would he forgive the bringing *Anadea* into his, whom he hated, not only for her narrow Circumstances, but also for an old Grudge between their Families. All this, though with an infinite Regret, did the tender Husband represent to his afflicted Wife, who, in spite of the Shocks it gave her Modesty, and conscious Virtue, to be look'd on as a Mistress, consented with a seeming Chearfulness; since to clear her Reputation must be the undoing of him, who was infinitely dearer to her than all other Considerations. But to make herself a little more at east than she had been, while amidst the daily Reproaches of those who pretended to be her Friends, and the Taunts and little Jests of Creatures, who pretended to value themselves on their undiscovered Vices, she proposed to retire: She told the *Count* that she would leave *Paris*, and changing her Name, make choice of some Place for her Abode where she was wholly a Stranger, till the Death of the relentless *Marquis*, or someother Accident, should happen, which should render it not a Misfortune to acknowledge her his Wife. She remember'd, that in her Journey to *Versailles*, she had gone through a very pleasant, but solitary Place, called *St. Clou*, and being unknown to everybody there, told him, she thought she could not make a fitter Choice. He was extremely pleased with the Design; and to strengthen her in it, added, that being unknown, he might visit her more frequently, and with greater Liberty, than he could hope to do in *Paris*, where there were so many busy Tongues who would be continually reporting everything to his Father. The Affair being thus settled, he took leave with less Dissatisfaction than he would have done, and went to the *Marquis* with more haste than he would have done, could he have guess'd at the Resolutions form'd against his Happiness.—He had no sooner enter'd the Room, where his Father with the utmost Impatience expected him, than he began to question him in this Manner:—I will not ask you, (*said he*,) whether you are now come determined in Obedience, or not:—I hope you are enough acquainted with your Duty to have no other Sentiments than those of Remorse for but a seeming Neglect of it:—But I would know, and I command you to inform me, what Reasons made you, not with Pleasure I expected, receive the Condescensions of Madam *De la Roche*. The *Count*, who had summoned on all his Courage for this Interview, readily replied, I am infinitely more amazed, my Lord, that you should feign Ignorance of what appear'd so plain, than you can beat my Behaviour:—My Reasons were not indeed so proper for my Tongue to reveal, at least, before that Lady; but I am certain that my Eyes have not sufficiently the power of Dissimulation, not to inform her my Dislike of her made me guilty, and will still keep me so, of Disobedience to you.—How! will keep you so?—(*cry'd the incens'd* Marquis.)—Pardon, my Lord, (*resumed he, throwing himself on his Knees,*) pardon your offending Son, who owns his Crime, but has not the Means of Reparation.—'Tis irresistible over- ruling Fate that contradicts your Will, and fixes in my Nature an Aversion so strong, as even your Commands, tho' ever sacred to me, have not the Power to shake.—'Tis false, (*replied the other, more enraged*) 'tis false: This counterfeit Humility may cheat a Girl; but used to me, gives double Provocation:—'Tis not your Aversion for Madam *De la Roche*, but Love for *Anadea*, embolden you thus to dare my Fury:—That Sorceress has bewitch'd you from your Duty, your Interest; but will her prostituted Charms repair your Loss of me?—Has she the Power to turn my Curses into Blessings? For Curses numberless, and only Curses shall be your Portion, if—He was proceeding, when the *Count*, to whom these Words were worse than Death, catching fast hold of his Knees, conjur'd his Pity and Forgiveness in Terms so tender, that had the Father been influenced by any part of that Good Nature his Son was so prodigiously stor'd with, he must have been moved by it: But fiery, obstinate, and cruel in his Disposition, he was so far from seeming touch'd, that finding there was no Hope of compassing his Intention either by Force or Perswasion, never was Fury more tempestuous than his: He branded *Anadea* with all the Names of Infamy that Malice can invent, and on his Son wished all the Plagues of Heaven and Earth. But young *Blessure*, fixed in Constancy, and steddy Faith, endured unmoved, tho' shocked, the dreadful Storm; and believing his Presence would be far from allaying it, begg'd leave to retire. No, (*said the* Marquis,) you shall find you are a Prisoner still; and with these Words, giving a great Stamp with his foot, in rushed five or six Fellows, entire Strangers to young *Blessure*, and who by their Looks, in any other Place than his Father's Lodgings, he would rather have taken for Assassines, than to be of any other Profession: But the *Marquis* leaving him no room for Conjecture, with a Look which sufficiently denoted the implacable Indignation of his Soul, cry'd our, It is to these Persons

I shall now resign the Authority I ought to have over you; and since you are weary of a Father's Power, will try how you can brook Obedience to that of others.—Go, (*continued he, if possible, more sternly than before,*) bear him to Banishment, and let me see his face no more, till Time and Penitence have wash'd away the Remembrance of his Crime.—This was all he said; and going hastily into his Closet, shut the Door after him, and would listen to nothing the *Count* was about to offer; who altogether unable to guess what was design'd for him, thought it no way blameable, when thus treated, to make resistance, and did it with such Fury, that he wounded two or three of these Fellows, before they could disarm him: But his Father's Servants coming in to their Assistance, at last he was over-powered, and forced into a Coach; which being guarded on each side, made it impossible for him to escape.—They made the best of their Way to the next Sea-Port town, whence, with the first fair Wind, they were to embark for what Place soever the Ship was bound; the *Marquis* having no other Design than to separate him from *Anadea*, not doubting but that Time and Absence would make an Alteration in his Humour.

That afflicted lady, in the mean Time, was preparing to leave *Paris*; and having heard of a Place, the agreeable Solitude of which seemed to suit her present Circumstances, was impatient to be gone: She waited for nothing but a Visit from *Blessure*, that she might inform him where she was going; but neither seeing nor hearing from him as she expected, she sent to his Lodgings, and at the Return of her Messenger, was inform'd of such News as was very near depriving her of her Senses: All his Retinue being removed, the People of the House said he was gone to Travel, to what Place they knew not; but that some of the *Marquis's* Servants, who came for his Baggage, had told them, That not being perfectly well pleas'd with a Match his Father had propos'd, and somewhat discontented at the Death of the Chevalier *De Semar*, killed by his Hand in a dishonourable Cause, he resolved in foreign Climes to endeavour to obliterate the Memory of what had been so prejudicial to his Fame and Peace of Mind at home. This was, indeed, the publick Rumour; and among all who heard it, there was not one who imagined his Departure had any other Motive than what was reported. *Anadea* doubted not of the Truth, and fell into so violent a Despair, that it is to be wonder'd at, that she sought not forcibly to rid herself of a Life, which promised her nothing but Misery: But she was reserved to know Misfortunes of a deeper Dye, than even her wild Fancy, black as it was, could represent; and not all the Horror she endur'd in a Belief that her dear *Blessure* was the falsest, basest, and most ungrateful of Mankind, not the fierce Convulsions, nor the Distraction which that Belief created in her, had the Power to drive the tortur'd Soul from its Habitation.—Now more than ever detesting all Society, and unable longer to endure a Place where she so much had suffer'd, so much had been betrayed, she pursued her Intentions of retiring to *St. Clou*.

The House she made choice of for her Abode, was about half a Mile distant from any other, and at least a Furlong, from the *Village*. It seem'd a Place cut out and fashion'd for Despair: The Situation of it was in a Vale, about a Bow-shot from the great Road, and encompassed with Trees of so vast a Height and Thickness, that a Passenger could not, without being appris'd of it, know there was any such Thing as a Habitation there. Behind it, there was a Wilderness altogether desolate and unfrequented; and it was there she passed the most part of her melancholy Hours, indulging Woe, and soothing Misery; and had this Way of Life continued, 'tis probable, by a long Habitude of numbing Grief, she might have grown at last as insensible as the Rocks and Woods to which she made her Moan.

But now the dreadful Time drew nigh, which was to consummate her Life, and her Misfortunes: She believ'd not that it was in the Power of Fate to make her more wretched than she was, and in the Height of Despair, had almost challenged Heaven to add another Woe to those she already felt!—But, alas! she was too soon convinced of the Folly of such an inconsiderate Daring!—She was not to leave the World without knowing, that there were Horrors to be felt infinitely beyond what yet she had any Notion of!

Returning one Evening from those shady Recesses, where she was accustomed to sooth her Sorrows, she was surprised with the Sight of several new Guests in the House:—He who appeared the Chief, was laid down on a Couch in the Parlour, and two or three Men seemed very busy about him; but how employed, or who they were, she was too much taken up with her usual Meditations, to enquire.—But she had not been above half an Hour in her Chamber, before the Woman of the House came up to her, and desired she would come down to Supper; which she was beginning to refuse, on the Account of those Strangers she had seen, when the good landlady, interrupting her, told her, that it was on the Account of those Strangers that she must not refuse.—The Person who you saw on my Couch, (*said she*) is a very great Man: His

Servants tell me, he is called the Marquis *De Blessure*.—Hap'ning to ride this Way, he had the Misfortune of a Fall from his Horse; and my House being the nearest, he was brought hither, and will stay till he has recover'd the Bruizes he receiv'd in this unlucky Accident.—He saw you pass through the Parlour, (*added she,*) and I believe is fallen in Love with you; for he has asked a thousand Questions about you, and begs, in finer Words than I know how to speak, that he may have the Honour of your Company.—Come, come, (*continued she, perceiving* Anadea *made no Answer*) you must not deny:—You don't know your own Interest, if you do:—Take my Word for it, you have snapped his Heart:—And I am seldom mistaken, especially in Things of this Nature.—You may make your Fortune, if you will. All the latter Part of this elegant Discourse was lost on her to whom it was addressed:—To hear the Maquis *De Blessure* was by so odd an Accident brought into the same House with her, and that he expressed a Liking to her, appear'd so whimsical an Effect of Fortune, that she could not Help thinking it promised something very extraordinary.—She knew he had never seen her as *Anadea*, and hop'd in the Character she now bore, she should be able to draw something from him in Conversation concerning his Son, who, in spite of his imagined Falshood, was still dear to her Soul. With the Help of this Consideration, the old Woman found it no very difficult Matter to perswade her to what she desir'd.—She had not been long in the *Marquis's* Presence, before she had reason to believe her Land-lady in the right: He had made a passionate Declaration of Love to her; and presuming on the Greatness of his Quality, and the supposed Meanness of hers, stood not on those Punctiolo's of Distance and Respect, which Lovers ordinarily do: He began to accompany his Words with Actions which were not at all pleasing to her:—He press'd her Hands, kiss'd, embraced her; and endeavouring to proceed to greater Liberties, she was oblig'd to repel him with Looks and Expressions, such as she never before had occasion to make use of.—The Manner of her Behaviour was such, as struck an Awe into him, as bold as he was; and though he was possessed with as violent a Desire as ever Man was, and had an equal Share of Pride, yet he desisted from treating her in the Fashion he had entertained her with all the humble Distance of the most beseeching Lover—the more he conversed with her, the more he found in her to admire:—He continued in the House; and everyday, ever Hour his Passion encreas'd, and at length was converted into so sincere a one, that he offered to marry her.—'Tis easy to imagine, she was extremely surprised at this Proposal from a Man of his Humour; but resolving to make her Advantage of it, for the Discovery of what concerned her so much to know;—How, my Lord, (*said she,*) is it possible that you can harbour a Design of that Nature?—You, I say, who, as the World reports, entail'd a lasting Load of Cruelty and Ingratitude on your only Son, by obliging him to quit the Woman he had sworn to love, only because her Fortune was inferior to his? Can you resolve to be guilty of that Folly yourself, which you were pleas'd to think so unpardonable in him? Had the Mistress of my Son, (*answered he,*) been possessed of half your Charms, I had not blam'd his Choice;—tho' (*added he*) there were other Reasons besides her Poverty, which render'd his loving her a Crime.

These Words gave *Anadea*, in the Character of a third Person, sufficient room to plead her own Cause; which she did so effectually, that he had little to say to excuse his Severity; and also by this Means artfully questioning him, as though in a careless Manner, found out the whole Truth how her Husband was disposed of.—The Discovery that he was not false, gave her a Pleasure, which none but those who tenderly love, and have felt the Tortures of that Love abused, can guess at.

She began now to hope her Woes were near a Period; and fancied that if she had it in her Power to reveal the Secret, he might now be prevailed on to pardon all.—She thought he could not condemn that Proof of Passion in his Son, which he had offered to give of his own; and that he would not like her less when known to be *Anadea*, than he did while he believed her a Person more inferior;—but she had given her Promise to *Blessure*, and durst not violate it:—She was, however, continually contriving which way she should evade it, and had certainly, at last, brought herself to confess the whole Affair, if not prevent by a Misfortune of the most dreadful kind that ever happen'd.

The old *Marquis* finding that not all his Offers worked the Effect he aimed at, and burning with Desire to enjoy her, resolved to compass it some way or other: In order to this hellish Intention, as they were at Supper, he found an Opportunity, unobserv'd by her, to mingle some Drops of *Opium* in her Drink; which making her more than ordinarily sleepy, she retired to Bed.—In the mean Time, with a Purse of Gold he prevail'd on the mercenary Temper of the Maid of the House, to leave the key of her Chamber in the Door; and when the Family were all gone to Rest, he softly stole on the unsuspected wretched *Anadea*, got into her Bed; and the curs'd Drug operating on her Senses for the

Purpose it was given, he accomplish'd the incestuous Joy before the Chain of Sleep dissolv'd.

The Lethargy she was in, was not, however, so strong, as to have the Power o'er Fancy:—Her dear *Blessure* was ever in her Thoughts; and at this moment, watchful Imagination brought him to her Arms.—In Sleep she prest him to her panting Breast; and the real Warmth of those Caresses she received, making her Dream more lively, she returned his Ardours with an Extasy too potent to the dull God's Restraint.—Unbounded Rapture broke thro' the Power of Art;—All her Senses regained at once their Liberty, and she awoke, to sleep no more.

The wild Confusion she was in, between the Effect of what she had taken, and her late Transport, prevented her for some Moments from the Knowledge of her Misfortunes: She was not immediately sensible whether what had past was Reality, or Illusion: But too soon recovering from that Stupidity which now was all that could render her any other than the most wretched Creature under Heaven, and feeling there was a real Substance in the Bed with her which still held her fact embraced, she gave a Shriek which might have alarmed People at a much greater Distance than those of the House were; which the *Marquis* endeavouring to silence by repeated Endearments, and all the Expressions of Tenderness his Passion could inspire, entirely convinced her she was indeed undone in the most dreadful and irreparable Manner.—Her Fury, he Madness, her Horror, was too mighty to vent itself in Words; but struggling with a Force which at that Time seem'd more than human, she unloosed herself from him, flew out of the Bed, and throwing herself on the Floor, cry'd out *Adultery!*—*Incest!*—*Damnation!*—and fell into a Fit so violent, so lasting, that the good Woman of the House, who her Shrieks had brought into the Room, believed she was dead.

The *Marquis* was so much alarmed at this uncommon Testimony of Despair, and the Words she had uttered, that he was wholly incapable either of contributing an Assistance to the bringing her to herself, or answering the Reproaches which the Land-lady, who was really a harmless honest Creature, vented for the Abuse he had offer'd,—but stood motionless, and wholly undressed all to his Shirt.—The base Wench, whose Avarice had been the Cause of this, was also there, and between her and her Mistress they laid the miserable *Anadea* on the Bed.—It was towards Morning before she recovered; and when she did, the *Marquis* standing just before her, watching her Return of

Sense, for an Explanation of what at present seemed so mysterious to him, the Sight of that detested Object, threw her again into the same Convulsions; and she had no longer an Interval of Speech, than to Shriek out again the horrid Sound of *Incest*. While they were thus employed, a prodigious Knocking was heard at the Door, which the Maid running down to know the Cause of, presently returned, and told her Mistress, there was a Gentleman who enquired for a young Lady lately come from *Paris*,—and that he would not be deny'd seeing her.—It cannot be our Lodger, (*said the Landlady*,) for I have often heard her say, she should have no Person come to visit her: But if it were she, you know she is not in a Condition for Company;—therefore go and dismiss him.—The Girl was about to do as she was order'd, when young *Blessure* entered the Chamber; for it was he, who having made his Escape from those to whom the *Marquis* had given the Charge of him, had rid Day and Night till he reached *St. Clou*. His Impatience to embrace his beloved *Anadea*, would not permit him to stay till the Return of the Servant: He followed her directly up Stairs, and perceiving the Disorder in which that distress'd Lady was, he ran to the Bed, and throwing himself on it by her, conjured her speak to him;—call'd her his Life, his Soul, his Angel, Goddess, all the endearing Names that Love can form, but among the rest, my charming *Anadea*, my Dear, my *lovely Wife*, were a thousand Times repeated.—The *Marquis* happening to stand in a part of the Room, from which the Light was pretty much shelter'd, had not yet been seen by his Son, felt a sudden Horror at the first mention of *Wife* and *Anadea*, and hearing them again and again repeated, was ready to fall into the same Condition with her whom he had ruin'd: But summoning all his Courage to be satisfy'd of the Truth, came forward to the Place where his Son was, and with as haughty an Accent as the inward Disorders of his Mind would give him leave, accosted him in the Manner:—You are returned, I find, (*said he*,) without Permission;—but if you hope my Pardon for this, or any former Acts of Disobedience, be quick, and ease my impatient Soul;—tell me who this Woman is, or how related to you.—Not all the Surprise and Grief the *Count* was in to find his Charmer in a Condition so different from what he expected, not all he felt at the Sight of his Father, in Place and Posture so astonishing, took from him the Power of paying him that Respect which he had been accustomed to do; and falling on his Knees, Proud to obey you, Sir, when Obedience is in my Power, I shall make no Scruple of confessing the virtuous *Anadea* is my Wife, and that this is she;—but why I find her in this Condition, is what I am fearful to demand:But—He was going on, when the *Marquis*, whose Eyes seem'd to shoot Fire, interrupted him, by crying, Is she your Wife! Your lawful married Wife! My Lord, she is (*resumed his Son*) my wedded Wife, lawfully married, and enjoyed:—And sooner would I have acknowledged it, if—Oh! it is now too soon, (*rejoined the* Marquis,) since too, too late to save us all from Ruin!—As the *Count* was about to beg an Interpretation of this ambiguous Expression, *Anadea* lifted up her Eyes, and the Strength of her Constitution having by this Time pretty well overcome her Disorders, she had the Use of her Senses enough to know her Husband immediately; and hearing the last Words the *Marquis* had said, rear'd herself up in the Bed, and taking hold of young *Blessure*, as though she meant to embrace him, snatched the Sword he wore by his Side, and plung'd it into her Bosom with such an incredible Strength and Swiftness, that had any of the Company been apprised of her Intent, it would have been scarce possible to have prevented her.—Now, (*said she*,) the shameful Story may be told!—living I could not bear it!—Hate me not after Death, my dear, dear Lord! and I have no more to ask!—With these Words she expir'd; and the almost distracted *Count* was scarce withheld from making the same fatal Use she had done of his Weapon:—But, wild to know the Source of his Misfortune, ask'd a thousand incoherent Questions;—which none presently answering, he raved about the Room like one utterly bereft of Reason.

The old *Marquis*, whose lawless and ungoverned Passion had occasion'd this Misfortune, still remained in a fixed Posture; but if we may guess by what ensued, felt at least an equal Share in those Agonies which so visibly possessed the *Count*.—Rouzing at length from his seeming Lethargy, he assumed as much as possible a Serenity of Countenance, and ordering his Son to attend him in his Chamber in half an Hour, left that dismal Scene to be filled up by him whose Griefs were too just for Controul.—The Woman of the House would fain have perswaded him from the Body; but he swore never to forsake it, but so long as to know the Cause of so shocking a Despair as that must be, which had influenced her gentle Soul to such an Act of Horror.

As he was uttering the most piteous Lamentations that Speech e'er form'd,—the Landlady, who stirred not far from him, heard a Pistol go off; and by the Sound, judged it was in the next Room.—Frighted and suspicious of the Truth, she started up, and cried,—Heaven grant there be not another Self-murder!—Let us go and see, my Lord, (*pursued she*;) I fear your Father's Desparation.

Young *Blessure*, to whom all appeared dark and mysterious, on the mention of his Father in that Manner, ran with the Woman to that Room whence the Noise had proceeded, and found the unhappy *Marquis* Shot through the Head.—A Paper lay by him of a Table writ by his own Hand, and directed to his Son,—containing the whole Transaction of this fatal Night,—blaming the *Count* for concealing his Marriage, but himself much more for giving way to Desires so injurious to Honour.

To go about to represent in what Manner the afflicted *Blessure* behaved at reading this amazing Discovery, would be to wrong a Grief which scarce Imagination can figure as it ought:—There was nothing that he omitted, to testify the most violent Despair, but laying violent Hands on his own Life; and even that he was but with Difficulty restrained from doing.—He buried both his Father and unfortunate Wife with all possible Solemnity.—Then declaring he had done with the World, made Sale of his vast Patrimony, and distributed it among the Poor; and retiring among the *Capuchins*, linger'd out three or four Years in wasting Sorrow, which at last consumed him; and he was interred by that dear Body, which his adverse Fate had denied him the Blessing of living with.

FINIS

A Note About the Author

Eliza Haywood (1693–1756) was an English novelist, poet, playwright, actress, and publisher. Notoriously private, Haywood is a major figure in English literature about whom little is known for certain. Scholars believe she was born Eliza Fowler in Shropshire or London, but are unclear on the socioeconomic status of her family. She first appears in the public record in 1715, when she performed in an adaptation of Shakespeare's *Timon of Athens* in Dublin. Famously portrayed as a woman of ill-repute in Alexander Pope's *Dunciad* (1743), it is believed that Haywood had been deserted by her husband to raise their children alone. Pope's account is likely to have come from poet Richard Savage, with whom Haywood was friends for several years beginning in 1719 before their falling out. This period coincided with the publication of *Love in Excess* (1719–1720), Haywood's first and best-known novel. Alongside Delarivier Manley and Aphra Behn, Haywood was considered one of the leading romance writers of her time. Haywood's novels, such as *Idalia: or The Unfortunate Mistress* (1723) and *The Distress'd Orphan; or Love in a Madhouse* (1726), often explore the domination and oppression of women by men. *The History of Miss Betsy Thoughtless* (1751), one of Haywood's final novels, is a powerful story of a woman who leaves her abusive husband, experiences independence, and is pressured to marry once more. Highly regarded by feminist scholars today, Haywood was a prolific writer who revolutionized the English novel while raising a family, running a pamphlet shop in Covent Gardens, and pursuing a career as an actress and writer for some of London's most prominent theaters.

A Note from the Publisher

Spanning many genres, from non-fiction essays to literature classics to children's books and lyric poetry, Mint Edition books showcase the master works of our time in a modern new package. The text is freshly typeset, is clean and easy to read, and features a new note about the author in each volume. Many books also include exclusive new introductory material. Every book boasts a striking new cover, which makes it as appropriate for collecting as it is for gift giving. Mint Edition books are only printed when a reader orders them, so natural resources are not wasted. We're proud that our books are never manufactured in excess and exist only in the exact quantity they need to be read and enjoyed.

Discover more of your favorite classics with Bookfinity™.

- Track your reading with custom book lists.
- Get great book recommendations for your personalized Reader Type.
- Add reviews for your favorite books.
- AND MUCH MORE!

Visit **bookfinity.com** and take the fun Reader Type quiz to get started.

Enjoy our classic and modern companion pairings!